THE CASTAWAYS

Also by the authors:
Bluesman 1,2,3, $8.95 each
Also from ComicsLit:
Brownsville, 18.95 hc, $12.95 pb
P&H: $3 1st item, $1 each addtl.

We have over 200 graphic novels in print,
write for our color catalog:
NBM
40 Exchange Pl., Ste 1308
New York, NY 10005
www.nbmpublishing.com

THE CASTAWAYS

Rob Vollmar
Pablo G. Callejo

Alameda Free Library
1550 Oak Street
Alameda, CA 94501

ISBN 10: 1-56163-492-1, hardcover
ISBN 13: 978-1-56163-492-7, hardcover
ISBN 10: 1-56163-493-X, paperback
ISBN 13: 978-1-56163-493-4, paperback

© 2007 Rob Vollmar & Pablo Callejo
Printed in China
3   2   1

ComicsLit is an imprint
and trademark of

NANTIER · BEALL · MINOUSTCHINE
Publishing inc.
new york

Chapter 1

MARCH 6TH, 1932. DADDY ALWAYS TALKED ABOUT THE TRAINS. I WAS FIVE THE FIRST TIME HE TOL' ME ABOUT THE BEND WHERE HE CAUGHT 'EM.

WE WERE SITTIN' UNDER THE BIG TREE ON THE SQUARE IN CABOOL AND I ASKED HIM...

"DADDY, WHERE YOU GONE TO ALL THE TIME?"

HE SAID, COOL AS YOU PLEASE...

BRUHT' HHHNNNNN

"UP AROUND THE BEND, S'WHERE THE TRAIN GOTTA SLOW DOWN LONG ENOUGH FOR ME TO WRASSLE A RIDE OUT OF IT."

FOOL I WAS, I BELIEVED HIM. IT WEREN'T THE LAST TIME...

I'VE STOOD AT THIS SPOT AND WATCHED THIS TRAIN GO BY ME WHAT MUSTVE BEEN A THOUSAND TIMES.

FIRST, WHEN I GOT A LITTLE OLDER, I'D GO TO SEE DADDY OFF TO THE ROAD.

WATCH HIM WRASSLE THE TRAIN. HE MADE IT LOOK SO EASY...

LATER, AFTER HE DISAPPEARED, I'D COME AND PRETEND I WAS WAITING FOR HIM.

IT WAS A LIE. I KNEW WHAT I WAS DOING.

I WAS REHEARSING THIS DAY IN MY MIND.

WHOSHHH!

MOMMA KNEW, TOO. SHE'D SIT AND CRY AND MAKE ME PROMISE OVER AND OVER THAT I'D STAY HOME AND NEVER JUMP THE TRAIN.

5123

I LIED AGAIN AND AGAIN BUT I DIDN'T KNOW IT THEN SO I DON'T THINK IT WAS A SIN.

IT WAS REALLY JUST A MATTER OF TIMING...

MOMMA'S GOT A WHOLE FLOUR SACK FULL OF THESE POSTCARDS. I RECKON SHE WON'T NOTICE THIS ONE GONE FOR A WHILE.

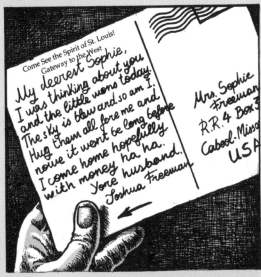

Come See the Spirit of St. Louis!
Gateway to the West

My deerest Sophie,
I was thinking about you and the little wons today. The sky is blew and so am I. Hug them all fore me and nowe it wont be long before I come home hopefully with money ha ha.
Yore husband,
Joshua Freeman

Mrs. Sophie Freeman
R.R. 4 Box 3
Cabool, Missou
U.S.A.

DADDY NEVER TOLD US WHERE HE WAS GOING 'CEPT BY THESE LITTLE ARROWS. WEST, THIS TIME, MAYBE NORTH THE NEXT.

THERE WAS NEVER ANY WARNING WHEN HE WAS ABOUT TO LEAVE. AFTER A SPELL OF BEING HOME, HE'D SAY...

"I'M HEADED INTO TOWN FOR SOME ERRANDS. ANYBODY NEEDIN' ANYTHING?"

I DIDN'T CATCH ON TO THE ROUTINE UNTIL I WAS ALMOST SEVEN. MOMMA WOULD PURSE HER LIPS AND NOT SAY NOTHING WHILE US KIDS WOULD ALL SCREAM FOR A LICORICE WHIP FROM THE DRUGSTORE.

HE'D JUST SMILE LIKE HE WAS PLANNING TO RETURN BEFORE THE SUN CAME DOWN, EVEN THOUGH IT'D LIKELY BE THREE, FOUR MONTHS 'FORE WE'D SEE HIM AGAIN.

UNTIL, FINALLY, HE JUST DIDN'T COME BACK.

THE RAIN LET UP AROUND 8:30 WHEN I FIGURED WE WAS PASSING BY MANSFIELD. MOMMA WON'T BE BACK FROM THE CAFE UNTIL ALMOST TWO.

IT'LL BE UP TO THE WIDOW TO LET HER KNOW WHAT I DONE...

SHE DIDN'T HAVE NO TROUBLE GIVING ME HARD NEWS SO I RECKON SHE'LL DO JUST FINE.

TUCKER, GRAB THE SLOP BUCKET AND FOLLOW ME OUT TO THE BARN. I'VE GOT SOME CHORES FOR YOU.

YES'M

THE WIDOW DIDN'T SAY NOTHING AS WE WALKED OUT TO THE BARN.

WHICH CAME AS NO GREAT SURPRISE CONSIDERIN' SHE HADN'T SAID TWENTY WORDS TO US KIDS IN THE FOUR MONTHS WE'D BEEN LIVIN' OUT AT HER FARM.

IT WEREN'T UNTIL WE GOT IN THE BARN THAT SHE EVEN LOOKED AT ME AND, EVEN THEN, I WAS HARDLY GRATEFUL.

I'LL FEED THE G—

TUCKER, DO I LOOK LIKE A WEALTHY WOMAN TO YOU?

HER WORDS STUNG BUT, ALL AT ONCE, I KNEW SHE WAS RIGHT. I WAS THIRTEEN AND DIDN'T HAVE NO RIGHT TO BE TUGGING AT MY MOMMA'S APRON STRINGS NO MORE...

IT'S TIME I GOT TO FARIN' FOR MYSELF. I'LL WORK ALL ALONG THE WAY AND SEND MONEY HOME AS I GO.

MOMMA WON'T WORRY SO MUCH ONCE SHE HEARS I'M ALRIGHT AND LIVING THE HIGH LIFE.

AND MAYBE, IF GOD'S TAKING ANY NOTICE OF ME AT ALL OUT HERE, I'LL FIND DADDY...

AND WE'LL BOTH GO BACK HOME...

...WHERE WE BELONG.

Chapter 2

THE TRAIN COMES TO REST IN THE SPRINGFIELD YARD JUST A LITTLE AFTER NOON.

I STAND THERE FOR WHAT SEEMS LIKE DAYS TRYING TO FIGURE OUT WHAT I'M GONNA DO NOW.

I KNOW THAT ALL THE TRAINS HEADIN' WEST LEAVE OUT OF ST. LOUIE.

TROUBLE IS, I GOT NO IDEA AS TO WHICH TRAIN GONNA TAKE ME THERE.

AND THOSE WORK CREWS KEEP MOVING CLOSER TO THE CAR I GOT MYSELF STASHED IN.

THE THOUGHT CROSSES MY MIND THAT THEY MIGHT NOT EVEN CHECK THIS CAR, SEEIN' HOW IT WAS EMPTY.

I'LL LEARN SOONER OR LATER NOT TO RELY ON BLIND CHANCE ANY MORE'N I HAS TO ...

I RECKON YOUR ELDERS TOLD YOU TO STAY AWAY FROM THEM COLOREDS, HUH?

NO, SIR. MY DADDY SAYS THAT GOD CREATED ALL MEN EQUAL AND SOME OF THE WOMEN, TOO!

IS THAT A FACT? WHAT'S YOUR NAME, LITTLE MAN?

TUCKER FREEMAN, SIR. AGE 13.

PLEASED TO MEET YOU, TUCKER. I'M ELIJAH HOPKINS AND I'M A SIGHT OLDER THAN THAT, I'M AFRAID.

LOOKS LIKE YOU GOT THAT CLEANED OUT RIGHTLY.

NOT MUCH CHANCE OF INFECTION IF YOU HAVE YOUR MOMMA CLEAN IT OUT WHEN YOU GET HOME.

MOMMMMMA! I-I'M NEVER G-GONNA SEE HER E-HE-VER AGAINNNN....

Chapter 3

Pablo
G.
Callejo
2002

ELIJAH TELLS ME ABOUT A PLACE, TUCKED DEEP IN A WOODED AREA NEAR THE EDGE OF TOWN WHERE ALL THE TRAMPS, OR 'BOS, AS HE CALLS THEM GO TO CAMP FOR THE NIGHT.

WE SET OFF TO WALKING IN SEARCH OF THIS PLACE 'ROUND ONE, WHEN THE SUN IS HIGH IN THE SKY AND A FELLER DON'T MUCH FEEL LIKE TALKING 'CAUSE HE'S THIRSTY.

NOW, JUDGING BY THE SUN AND THE GROWL IN MY GUT, IT'S GOTTA BE CLOSE TO FIVE.

'LIJAH, YOU SURE YOU KNOW WHERE WE'RE AT?

I WONDER WHAT MOMMA IS THINKING ABOUT ME RIGHT NOW?

NOW LOOKIE WHAT WE GOT HERE, OH YE OF LITTLE FAITH.

I GOT PLENTY OF FAITH, 'LIJAH, BUT MY BELLY IS BACKSLIDING QUICK. WHAT DID YOU FIND?

THIS HERE, TUCKER, IS A GENUINE SIGN FROM UP ABOVE. YOU SEE THAT THERE?

IS IT FOOD OR A PLACE TO SIT DOWN?

THIS HERE TRIANGLE MEANS BOTH AND THE ARROW PRETTY MUCH SPEAKS FOR ITSELF.

THAT MEANS THE JUNGLE SHOULD BE RIGHT HERE NEARBY.

WHEN WE GET THERE, YOU STAY CLOSE BY ME AND DON'T TELL NOBODY NOTHING 'LESS I SAY IT'S ALRIGHT, YOU HEAR?

SURE, 'LIJAH. I WON'T SAY NOTHING TO NO ONE.

SEEIN' AS HOW I DON'T KNOW YOU TOO WELL YET, I FEEL OBLIGED TO ASK. ARE YOU THE THIEVING KIND, TUCKER?

G-GOSH, NO, 'LIJAH. MY DADDY TOLD ME THAT STEALING WAS AKIN TO MURDER IN HIS MIND, S'FAR AS SINS GO...

THAT'S GOOD. I CAN'T HELP YOU NONE IF YOU GET CAUGHT IN THE JUNGLE STEALING FROM A FELLOW 'BO.

DON'T WORRY NONE, THOUGH, THERE IS GONNA BE MORE TO EAT TONIGHT THAN YOU GOT BELLY TO FILL.

I'M NOT SAYING THAT THERE ISN'T A SPECIAL KIND OF HUNGRY WHERE YOU STOP ASKING QUESTIONS 'BOUT RIGHT AND WRONG.

BUT ONLY YOU'LL KNOW WHEN YOU HAVE... ARRIVED.

* HUF * I'LL CROSS THAT BRIDGE * HUF * WHEN I COME TO IT. I JUST WOULDN'T FEEL RIGHT ABOUT * HUF * TAKING SOMETHING WITHOUT PERMISSION.

LOOKIE THERE, TUCKER! JUST LIKE THE SIGN SAID...

HOBO JUNGLE, DEAD AHEAD!

LAND O' GOSHEN! I NEVER SEEN SO MANY TRAMPS IN ONE PLACE...

CAREFUL WHO YOU CALL A TRAMP, SON. THERE'S THREE TYPES OF MEN OUT ON THE ROAD...

THE FIRST AND MOST NOBLE IS THE HOBO. A 'BO TRAVELS AROUND ON THE RAILROADS WE BUILT AND EARN HIS OWN.

A TRAMP, ON THE OTHER HAND, TRAVELS BY THE EASIEST MEANS AVAILABLE AND BEGS FOR HIS KEEP- STEALING WHEN HE AIN'T EVEN HUNGRY.

LAST IN LINE'S THE BUM WHO DON'T GO NOWHERE AND DON'T DO NOTHING BUT PUT OUT HIS HAND WHEN FOLK'S WALK BY 'CAUSE HE'S USUALLY TOO HUNGRY AND SICK TO STEAL.

HOW DO THEY SURVIVE?

THEY DON'T. A BUM'S JUST WAITING FOR LIFE TO COME 'ROUND AND KILL HIM OFF.

NOW, YOU WAIT HERE A SECOND, TUCKER. I THINK I SEE THE MAN WE NEED TO TALK TO.

I IGNORE THE PANIC THAT STARTS TO RISE UP ON THE BACK OF MY NECK AS I SEE ELIJAH WALKING OFF, EVEN IF IT'S JUST FOR A SECOND.

SUDDENLY, I GOT VISIONS IN MY HEAD OF DADDY, LAYING ON THE STREETS OF SOME FARAWAY CITY, UNABLE TO DO FOR HIMSELF OR GET HOME.

RELYING ON CHARITY FROM STRANGERS.

STRICKEN DOWN BY PARALYSIS OR BLINDED. WAITING FOR LIFE TO COME AND KILL HIM OFF.

IS THAT WHAT I GOT WAITING FOR ME, TOO?

SAY, THERE, LITTLE BIRD? YOU LOOK LIKE YOU NEED A FRIEND!

WHA-?

HAROLD JACKSON, SON, HAROLD JACKSON, BUT ALL THE JUNGLE FOLK CALLS ME HAWK. YOU BANG UP YOUR KNEE?

IT'S FINE. I-I'M FINE, MR. HAWK. I'M JUST WAITING FOR SOMEBODY.

IT AIN'T RIGHT THAT A YOUNGIN' BE LEFT IN THE JUNGLE WITHOUT PROPER CARE, SON. YOU GOT ALL TYPES LURKING 'ROUND HERE...

WHY, THEY EVEN LET THE COONS EAT WITH THE DECENT FOLK.

Chapter 4

AFTER DINNER, I START TO FEEL THE DAY DRAGGING AT MY HEELS, THOUGH IT CAIN'T BE NO LATER THAN HALF PAST EIGHT OR SO...

HOW COULD IT ONLY BE LAST NIGHT SINCE I WAS GETTIN' READY FOR BED, KNOWIN' I WOULD NEVER SEE MOMMA OR THE YOUNGINS AGAIN?

ONLY THIS MORNING THAT I NEARLY RIPPED MY ARM OFF CATCHING MY FIRST TRAIN AND A SLOW MOVER AT THAT?

EVEN NOW, I PROBABLY WOULDN'T EVEN BE ALIVE IF IT WEREN'T FOR MEETING ELIJAH...

WHAT IF SOMETHING BAD HAPPENS TO HIM?

WHO'S GONNA PROTECT ME THEN?

I WONDER IF MOMMA FEELS LIKE CRYIN' RIGHT NOW, TOO?

YOU STICK THAT BOTTOM LIP OUT MUCH FURTHER AND A BIRD'S GONNA LEAVE THE WORST PART OF HISSELF THERE FOR ALL TO SEE...

?

I-IT'S MY LIP AND I'LL WEAR IT HOW I PLEASE AND THANK YOU.

I RECKON THAT IT'S EVERY MAN'S RIGHT TO FEEL SORRY FOR HIMSELF WHEN TIMES DEMAND.

AWW, I AIN'T GOT IT SO BAD...

NO, I 'SPOSE WE AIN'T. WE GOT A HOT MEAL AND A CLEAR NIGHT TO SLEEP THROUGH IN A SAFE PLACE.

NOW, LET'S SEE IF I GOT ENOUGH BUTT ENDS IN HERE TO MAKE US A CIGARETTE.

OH, WE AIN'T GOT TO SCRAPE NOTHING, 'LIJAH!

THAT'S GOOD 'CAUSE IT SEEMS ALL I GOT IN THIS HERE IS GOOD INTENTIONS...

ELIJAH DON'T SAY NOTHING ELSE AND IT DOESN'T TAKE MUCH STARING INTO THE PEACEFUL NIGHT SKY TO SEND THE DAY'S TROUBLE PACKING...

LAST THING I HEAR 'LIJAH SAY 'FORE I DRIFT OFF IS "TUCKER, DON'T SLEEP TO HARD, NOW. THAT TRAIN IS LEAVING BEFORE THE SUN IS UP AND WE GOT SOME TRAVELIN' TO GET THERE".

SOME TIME IN THE NIGHT, I HAVE A DREAM.

I'M WALKING DOWN THE ROAD BETWEEN OUR OLD HOUSE AND TOWN...

WHEN UP IN THE DISTANCE, I SEE SOMEONE ELSE WALKING.

AND ALL THE SUDDEN, I KNOW IT'S HIM...

THEY ARE STILL ECHOING IN MY EARS WHEN I AWAKEN...

C'MON, TUCKER, GET UP. WE GOT GROUND TO COVER...

MOMMA?

WE ALREADY DONE COVERED THIS ONCE, JUNIOR. I AIN'T YOUR MOMMA!!

NOW, GET YOUR THINGS GATHERED AND LET'S MOVE!

WHAT DO YOU THINK ABOUT THAT KNEE?

I DON'T KNOW, 'LIJAH. IT IS STILL SORE, YET.

WELL, YOU CAIN'T TAKE THAT WALKING STICK NO FURTHER THAN THE TRAIN, ANYHOWS.

YOU COULDN'T CATCH A BUTTERFLY WITH THAT BUM LEG AND A CANE, LET ALONE A TRAIN IN THE DARK...

YOU SHOULD HAVE IT WALKED OUT GOOD ENOUGH FOR JUMPING BY THE TIME WE REACH THE TRACKS.

IS IT FAR?

NOT FAR 'T ALL BUT WE GOTTA MOVE, SON...

..."CAUSE THE TRAIN DON'T WAIT FOR NOBODY".

"THE TRICK IS TO GET OURSELVES ONTO THAT TRAIN WHEN IT'S MOVING TOO FAST TO STOP BUT SLOW ENOUGH TO CATCH"

ALL AWAY DOWNSIDE!!

"FAR ENOUGH AHEAD OF THE BULLS LAGGING BEHIND BUT FAR ENOUGH BEHIND THE BULL UP FRONT THAT HE CAN'T STOP US".

"OR, IN THE WORST CASE, SHOOT US!"

ALRIGHT, THERE HE GOES. I'M COUNTIN' TO FIVE AND THEN WE GO. ONE!

IT DOESN'T TAKE BUT TWO TICKS OF THE CLOCK FOR ME TO REMEMBER THAT SICK FEELING IN MY GUT I GOT YESTERDAY WHEN I HEARD THE TRAIN BREAKING AROUND THE BEND.

I TRY TO STAY FOCUSED ON ELIJAH BUT BETWEEN BEING HALF ASLEEP AND SCARED OUT OF MY MIND FOR TWO DAYS NOW, I--

FIVE!

UT!

?

OWW!

HEY, YOU BUMS! STOP!!

CHARLIE, WE GOT 'LOADERS!!

TUCKER, GRAB MY HAND!

GOOD LORD, DON'T LET ME SLIP AND FALL UNDER THIS TRAIN!

THAT'S JUST NO WAY FOR A BOY TO DIE...

Chapter 5

♪ "TALK ABOUT SUFFERIN' HERE BELOW AND LET'S KEEP FOLLOWING JESUS..." ♪

♪ "TALK ABOUT SUFFERIN' HERE BELOW AND LET'S KEEP FOLLOWING JESUS..." ♪

OH, CAIN'T YOU HEAR IT MOTHER AND DON'T YOU WANT TO GO?

AND LEAVE THIS WORLD OF TRIAL AND SUFFERIN' HERE BELOW... ♪

'LIJAH, I THOUGHT YOU WAS ANGELS AT FIRST...

LET'S HOPE THE LORD GOT SOMETHING BETTER TO LISTEN TO FOR ALL ETERNITY THAN MY CRACKED THROAT!

HOW DO YOU FEEL, TUCKER?

EVERYTHING HURTS...

DID I GET SHOT?

YEP, AND IF IT HAD BEEN BUCKSHOT, YOU'D BE IN A WORLD OF MISERY RIGHT NOW IF NOT BLED TO DEATH ON TOP OF THIS HERE TRAIN.

AS IT STANDS, TODAY, THEY WERE USING ROCK SALT...

WE WASN'T EVEN WORTH A REAL SHELL...

YOU ARE GOING HOME, TUCKER...

AND THERE IT IS, JUST LIKE HE SAYS.

HOME... OR PURT NEAR IT.

I DONE TOLD YOU, 'LIJAH, I GOT NO HOME ANYMORE.

THERE'S NO POINT LINGERIN' WHERE A FELLER AIN'T WANTED...

THAT'S WHAT YOU KEEP TELLING ME, ANYWAY, BUT THAT'S NOT WHY YOU RAN AWAY, IS IT, TUCKER?

'CAUSE IF YOUR DADDY IS MISSIN' AND YOUR MOMMA DIDN'T WANT YOU TO GO, THEN THE ONLY ONE WITH ANY BUSINESS LEFT TO RUN YOU OFF WAS YOU!

NOOOOOOO!

I DIDN'T WANT TO GO! I-IT WAS THE WIDOW!!

"BOYS, A BLUE RIBBON'D BE DANDY IF WE WAS AT THE COUNTY FAIR, BUT WHAT I COULD REALLY DO WITH IS SOME HELP WITH THE DISHES AFTER LUNCH".

I'D HAVE BETTER CHANCES AT TRYING TO TALK THE WIDOW OUTTA GOIN' TO WEDNESDAY SERVICES...

... THAN I WOULD CONVINCIN' THE ALDERMAN HICKS TO ROLL UP HIS FANCY SLEEVES AND SCRAPE DRIED EGGS OF THIS MORNING'S PLATES.

AND WE ALL KNOW THAT THERE'S JUST NO TALKING TO THE WIDOW.

MOMMA! MOMMA!

THE NEXT MORNING.

NOW, WHAT'S THIS I HEAR ABOUT A MISSING—

SOPHIE, WHAT'S HAPPENED?

IT'S MY BOY, TUCKER, SHERIFF. HE'S TURNED UP MISSING...

I CAN TELL THAT YOU ALREADY TURNED OVER THE COUNTRYSIDE LOOKING FOR HIM LAST NIGHT.

WHEN'S THE LAST ANYONE SEEN HIM?

TUCKER WOKE US UP LIKE NORMAL 'ROUND DAYBREAK AND GOT US READY FOR SCHOOL.

HE WAS HEADED INTO THE BARN TO MILK THE GOAT FOR OTIS JOHN'S BREAKFAST WHEN WE LEFT OR SO HE SAID.

I JUST KNOW THAT THE WIDOW HAS GOT SOMETHING TO DO WITH HIM UP AND DISAPPEARIN'.

IT WAS ALL SHE COULD DO TO KEEP HERSELF FROM GRINNIN' THE WHOLE TIME I WAS THERE.

NOW DON'T TAKE THIS WRONG, SOPHIE, BUT AIN'T IT POSSIBLE THAT THE BOY GOT RESTLESS LIKE HIS PA AND JUST WENT OFF WANDERING A BIT?

I MEAN, HE IS JOSHUA'S BOY.

HE'S **OUR** SON, MINE AND JOSHUA'S, JOHN, AND I DIDN'T RAISE HIM LIKE THAT.

WE DON'T RUN AWAY FROM OUR FAMILIES...

WE—WE DON'T ABANDON TH-THOSE WHO NEED US AND LOVE US...

W-WE'RE FAMILY. IT M-MEANS SOMETHING.

DAMN IT, IT MEANS SOMETHING.

DON'T CRY MAMA...

End

EPILOGUE

The story that you have just read (or are considering reading in skimming this here epilogue to see if we are your kind of folks) is a work of fiction. To the best of my knowledge, no one ever tore down that hateful sign that was posted on the outskirts of Cabool, Missouri (and many other towns) until it was finally taken down for good...a date that eluded my own research on the topic.

But, it was definitely there and, as a result, just like Tucker, my grandmother, Ruth Marie Bradley, who was born and lived in Cabool, did not, by her own admission, even meet a person of African-American descent until she was in her twenties (the 1950s). Lucky for me, her natural sense of tolerance was well-developed by that time from years of hard but honest living, not only making do with which she had, but also providing for others. In time, she instilled in my mother those same values and so, for reasons too diverse for breezy consideration and fates too kind for scrutiny, I was raised among the well-publicized intolerance and occasional willful ignorance of the Mid-South with a hand taught to shake, not to make a fist. My grandmother also shared stories with me about her childhood, stories that would eventually settle into myth after we left the countryside for the city during the lean Reagan years. Her father was, in addition to being a war veteran and a dedicated provider for his family, a hobo. He was a migrant worker, distinguished from the immigrant populations that still work those same lush California fields today

only by time and casual ethnicity. This lifestyle, of riding the rails to get to where the work was, was common to many uneducated men from all over the region and wouldn't, until the Great Depression, guarantee a feller a bad lot for himself, either, if he was diligent.

Despite this mythological inheritance, the seed for THE CASTAWAYS was born out of my viewing a marvelous documentary called RIDING THE RAILS that details the lives of some 250,000 children and teenagers that left home, willingly and/or otherwise, during the Great Depression, hopping trains in search of their fortunes that often never came. The conflicts that led these kids to test their mettle against a largely unwelcoming world instantly cried out for closer consideration and so, with some more research materials under my arm, I went back as close to the source as I could go.

When I first told my grandmother about my plans to write this story as a comic book, I got a long moment of silence followed by her perfunctory, "Well, Gawd..."

But, she quickly warmed up to my incessant questions about "the old days," reveling, maybe for the first time, in the chance to tell her story, one she often commented on as being dull or somehow without merit before losing herself again in enthusiastic reminiscence. I kept taking notes. One day while we were talking, I was frothing at the mouth about the socio-economic conditions in the rural South during the late Twenties when Grandma stopped me short, asking, "Robbie, why was Daddy gone so much when I was small?" I stammered for a moment before finally settling on, "It was the only way he knew how to make money when times got hard."

Strangely, she seemed satisfied enough with that, as if I had somehow answered a question that had been on her mind for a very long time. I'm not even sure that what I said was as important as the fact that someone had finally recognized her loss.

Less than a year later, three months before the first serialized installment of THE CASTAWAYS was due to hit the shelves, Ruthie was overcome by an aggressive brain tumor and, after a month of fighting, she finally passed the veil in my home, surrounded by her family.

I remember at one point in her struggle, she swam up to consciousness from beneath the sea of morphia to tell us that a black man had been there and he was going to take her to St. Louis. Distracted as I was at the time by my own intense grief, I didn't see the connection between her vision and the story I was writing, largely drawn from the fertile soil of her life but now, in reflection, maybe I understand.

I can only hope that Elijah put her on the train to Memphis, instead, so she could get back home...where she belonged.

Thank you again for your kind patronage. Y'all come back now, you hear?

ROB VOLLMAR

Sketchbook